I Can Read Comics introduces children to the world of graphic novel storytelling and encourages visual literacy in emerging readers. Comics inspire reader engagement unlike any other format. They ask readers to infer and answer questions, like:

1. What do I read first? Image or text?
2. Why is this word balloon shaped this way, and that word balloon shaped that way?
3. Why is a character making that facial expression? Are they happy, angry, excited, sad?

From the comics your child reads with you to the first comic they read on their own, there are **I Can Read Comics** for every stage of reading:

Simple stories for shared reading.

Engaging stories for children reading on their own.

Complex stories for independent readers.

The magic of graphic novel storytelling lies between the gutters. Unlock the magic with...

I Can Read Comics!

Visit **ICanRead.com** for information on enriching your child's reading experience.

I Can Read Comics Cartooning Basics

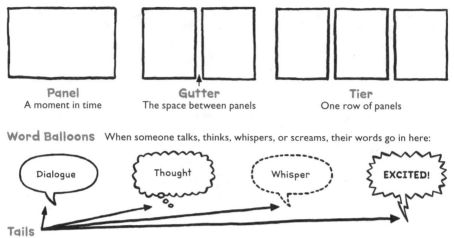

Panel
A moment in time

Gutter
The space between panels

Tier
One row of panels

Word Balloons When someone talks, thinks, whispers, or screams, their words go in here:

Dialogue

Thought

Whisper

EXCITED!

Tails
Point to whoever is talking / thinking / whispering / screaming / etc.

A quick how-to-read comics guide:

In a **panel**, read the text on the **left** first.

Then, read the text on the **right**.

On a page, **start** here, in the **top left** corner!

After that, read the panel immediately to the **right**.

When you're done up there, come down here and read **this** panel **next**!

ME NEXT! ME NEXT!

You're almost there...

YOU MADE IT! You just read a comic page!

YAY!

Remember to...
Read the text along with the image, paying close attention to the character's acting, the action, and/or the scene. Every little detail matters!

No dialogue? No problem!
If there is no dialogue within a panel, take the time to read the image. Visual cues are just as important as text, so don't forget about them!

To Giuseppina —S.R.

HarperAlley is an imprint of HarperCollins Publishers.
I Can Read® and I Can Read Book® are trademarks of HarperCollins Publishers.

Fish and Worm
Copyright © 2023 by Sergio Ruzzier

ISBN 978-0-06-329035-8 (trade bdg.) — ISBN 978-0-06-329034-1 (pbk.)

Book design by Maddy Price
23 24 25 26 27   LB   10 9 8 7 6 5 4 3 2 1   First Edition

an Read!
Comics

FISH and WORM

by Sergio Ruzzier

HARPER
alley

An Imprint of HarperCollins Publishers

It was lunchtime,
but Fish didn't want
to eat.

And you will get
a belly ache.